Mauby and the Hurricane

PETER LAURIE

Illustrated by H. ANN DODSON

MACMILLAN CARIBBEAN

Mauby the cat crept along the branch of the mango tree, stalking her prey, a skinny brown rat nibbling on a mango.

She was no longer a fat farm cat, afraid of heights. She was a fierce leopard in the jungle of Africa, waiting to pounce on her unsuspecting victim.

The branch bent beneath her weight. Mauby wobbled but hung on. The rat stopped eating, looked up, and turned around.

Mauby gave the rat a ferocious stare. That would scare him. The rat stared back, and then started to crawl along the branch towards her.

'Hey, what's going on here?' thought Mauby. 'I'm supposed to be chasing you.'

3

As the rat got closer, Mauby panicked, tried to turn around, looked down and lost her grip.

She fell, twisting and screaming, into the trough of water under the tree.

4

As she scrambled out of the trough, coughing and spitting water, Mauby heard shrieks of laughter. Bongo the dog, Myra the cow, and Shakes the black belly sheep stood around the trough, laughing. Up in the mango tree, the blackbird cackled.

'Great dive!' sniggered Bongo.

'Yeah,' cawed Tiki-Tak the blackbird, 'but I thought cats were supposed to land on their feet, not their head.'

Shakes bleated and shook with laughter. Bongo howled, sending some nearby chickens scattering.

'Stop blubbering, you stupid sheep!' Mauby picked on the animal she feared least. Bongo could bite her, Myra could butt her, and Tiki-Tak could peck her. But Shakes was harmless, not to mention a stupid nag.

These friends all lived together on a farm in the foothills of a small island in the Caribbean.

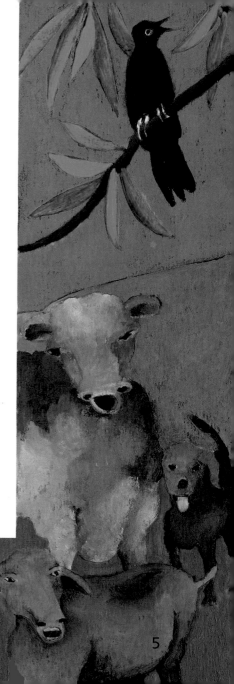

5

The other animals liked and admired Mauby, because she had once risked her own life to save Myra's calf, but they couldn't help teasing her. She was fat, lazy, awkward, and thought she was smarter than everyone else.

Suddenly they heard a sharp hoot from the old Silk Cotton tree. They looked up and saw Boo the owl peering down severely at them from his hole in the trunk.

'If you have all quite finished playing the fool, perhaps you will pay attention to what I have to say.'

They grew quiet. No one was more respected on the farm than Boo. He was wise and could see into the future.

'You are all in great danger. The farm is in great danger.'

You could have heard a pin drop in the silence that followed Boo's words.

'D-D-Danger?' stammered Shakes.

'Don't interrupt! Don't you use the senses the good Lord gave you? Look around you. Smell. Listen.'

Nervously the animals on the ground looked around them, sniffing, ears twitching.

Tiki-Tak, up in the mango tree, was the first to speak. 'I don't see anything, I don't hear anything.'

7

'Precisely,' said Boo.

'I don't get it,' said Bongo.

'Ooohh!' hooted Boo impatiently. 'Look at the trees. Not a leaf is moving. Look at the smoke from the bonfire down the hillside. It's going straight up in the air.'

'That's because there is no wind,' said Myra.

They suddenly noticed how totally still and quiet it was. Not a cloud moved in the sky. The sea, way below them in the distance, was flat as a lake.

'Oh no!' cried Mauby. The danger had suddenly dawned on her.

'Yes,' said Boo. 'You've forgotten the old rhyme I taught you.

June too soon,
July stand by,
August a must,
September remember,
October all over.'

'Oh yes,' screeched Tiki-Tak, 'the Hurricane season.'

'Correct. And what month is this?'

'August!' they all shouted.

'Exactly. A Hurricane is going to hit the island any moment!'

'B-B-But,' stuttered Shakes, 'Farmer Hunte and his wife have gone to market. And that's on the other side of the island. They'll never get back in time. What'll happen to us?'

'You're on your own. That's why you have to act now, and act together. You, Mauby, must be the leader.'

'Me! Why me?' complained Mauby.

'Because I say so. Besides, you need the exercise,' hooted Boo.

'But what do you want me to do, Boo?'

'You'll figure it out, Mauby. In the meantime I have things to do.' Boo disappeared into his hole in the tree trunk.

All the other animals looked at Mauby, waiting for her to tell them what to do.

'OK,' said Mauby, 'the house is all shut up, so all we have to do is get the animals into the barn. That's the safest place to be in the Hurricane. Shakes, you go and round up the other sheep on the lower pasture. Myra, you call in the other cows and the two horses in the upper field. Tiki-Tak, you warn the ducks and geese down by the pond. Bongo, you get the pigs out of their sty, and I'll chase the chickens into the barn and make sure there's enough food and water for everyone.'

While the other animals went off to do their tasks, Mauby chased the squawking chickens into the barn. There was hay for the sheep, horses and cows. She tore open a bag of feed for the fowls and a bag of sweet potatoes for the pigs. There was plenty of water for everyone.

Mauby looked around the barn. It was built of heavy beams with solid planks of wood. The roof was made of galvanised sheets of metal nailed on to the rafters. The barn looked as if it could withstand high winds.

As the excited farm animals began to trickle into the barn, either singly or in small groups, the wind began to blow. The sky filled with dark whirling clouds. Just as Bongo pushed the doors shut behind the last straggling pig, a brilliant flash of lightning zigzagged out of the sky, followed by an ear-splitting clap of thunder. The rain came pelting down.

The animals huddled together, screaming at the top of their voices.

'Shut up!' shouted Mauby, jumping up on to a bale of hay. 'Don't panic! We are quite safe in the barn. Now, is everyone here? Please check carefully.'

All the animals looked around at each other and started counting and calling names.

Soon the barn was filled with neighing, mooing, cackling, bleating and oinking. The din was deafening.

'Quiet!' Mauby shouted again.

Suddenly Shakes gave a loud bleat. 'Zoë and her lamb are missing! I told her to follow me. She is so hard-eared. She never listens to me. I told her … aieee!' Bongo had just nipped Shakes's backside. It was the only way to stop her talking.

'Okay, Shakes,' said Mauby. 'Calm down. Where did you last see Zoë?'

'She was in the lower pasture, under the dunks tree. I thought she was coming behind …'

'She is all right,' came a voice from up in the rafters. It was Boo. 'The lightning scared the lamb and it ran off. They're together in the hollow by the breadfruit tree. Mauby, I suggest you and Bongo go fetch them. But be careful. The wind is quite strong.'

As Mauby, followed by Bongo, slipped through the door, the wind bowled her over. Clinging with her claws to the ground, she dragged herself upright. Bongo, using all his strength, leaned into the wind. They staggered slowly out into the pasture and over to the breadfruit tree, which was swaying wildly in the wind. The rain almost blinded them

Huddled under the tree were Zoe and her terrified lamb.

Bongo grabbed the lamb by the scruff of its neck while Mauby tried to calm Zoë. They then set off for the barn with Bongo and the lamb in the lead, followed by Zoë. Mauby brought up the rear.

Suddenly Mauby heard a faint mewing. She stopped. Maybe the wind was playing tricks on her. She started walking again. This time the mewing was louder. It came from the casuarina tree she was passing under. Mauby looked up. Stuck halfway up the tree was Patches, the kitten from the farm next door, clutching a branch.

'Bongo! You go on ahead with Zoë. I'll get Patches.'

16

Mauby was afraid of heights. But she had no choice. Boo had made her the leader. She had to rescue the kitten. Slowly she clawed her way up the trunk until she reached the branch which Patches was holding on to for dear life.

'Help!' mewed the kitten. The tree was shaking so violently that Mauby could barely hold on.

'You silly little thing,' shrieked Mauby above the howling of the wind. 'Don't you know better than to climb up a tree in a Hurricane?'

'How are we going to get down?' blubbered Patches.

'Good question,' replied Mauby. Mauby suddenly realised that there was no way she could climb back down the trunk by herself, far less with a kitten in her mouth. The wind was shrieking through the tree.

'Quick! Hold onto my back.' The kitten let go of the branch and grabbed Mauby's back with claws and teeth. Just then a gust of wind tore fiercely through the tree, sending Mauby whirling into the air with the kitten on her back. Mauby did what her instincts told her to do. She spread her feet wide and tried to stay upright. Somehow she managed to glide with the wind and landed with a thump on the pasture next to Bongo and Zoë, startling them.

'Did you see me, Bongo? I was flying.'

'That's not flying,' sneered Bongo, 'that's falling with style. Come on, let's get inside the barn.'

Just then Gamps the horse came trotting out of the barn,

'Myrtle the young hen is missing. The ducks say she was in the pond.' shouted Gamps.

'That stupid Myrtle,' snorted Mauby, 'she thinks she is a duck. Why am I surrounded by silly fools? Okay, I'll go and get her. But this is the last animal I'm rescuing. It's dangerous out here.' Bongo with the lamb in his mouth, Gamps with Patches on his back, and Zoe hurried to the safety of the barn.

A dazzling flash of lightning forked down and struck the casuarina tree, splitting it in two. Peals of thunder clattered above the farm. A sheet of galvanised roofing hurtled through the air. Shrubs and branches of trees tumbled across the pasture.

'How am I ever going to get to the pond? This is worse than an obstacle course,' said Mauby.

'Maybe I can help.' The deep voice came from under a clump of khus khus grass. Warri the ancient tortoise poked her head out.

'You?' exclaimed Mauby, 'How can you help?'

'Well, I'm very heavy and low to the ground so the wind can't blow me over. And my shell is tough. You crawl under me and I'll shelter you as I run to the pond.'

'Run? I never heard of a tortoise running. Let's face it, Warri, you are not the fastest creature on God's earth. By the time we get to the pond the Hurricane will be over.'

'Well, if that's your attitude …' and Warri drew in her head and retreated under the bush.

A violent gust of wind blew Mauby off her feet.

'Okay, sorry. I accept your offer of help,' and Mauby crawled beneath the massive body of Warri, who stood up as high as she could off the ground. Warri set off for the pond at full speed. Mauby was surprised how fast a tortoise could move.

The duck pond, full to the brim, had spilled over. The water was rushing in a stream down the ditch that led to the river. Mauby spied Myrtle in the midst of the stream, squawking at the top of her voice and flapping her wings madly.

Leaving the shelter of Warri, Mauby crawled down the shallow side of the ditch to the stream's edge. Sheltered from the full blast of the wind, she raced along the ditch. But as fast as she ran, she could not catch up with Myrtle.

All of a sudden the river came into view. Swollen with water from the hills, it was tearing along wildly. The muddy water swirled and tossed about. The banks of the river were crumbling. Shrubs and trees fell into the foaming water.

Mauby made a frantic effort to reach Myrtle before the little hen was swept out into the river.

In vain.

The stream hurled Myrtle into the torrent of the river. But just as Mauby was giving up all hope, she saw that Myrtle had miraculously collided with part of the roof of a house and had wedged herself in a hole between two shingles. For the time being Myrtle was safe, but Mauby knew that wouldn't last long. The roof would soon be torn apart by the rushing river. Mauby had to rescue her. But how? It was impossible.

She felt a sharp tug on her tail and heard a familiar voice.

'Well, what is our brave cat up to now?' It was Sly One, the mongoose, pushing his long nose out of a hole in the ground under a horse nicker bush.

Mauby had mixed feelings about Sly One. He always pretended to help her but ended up tricking her. Each time Mauby fell for his tricks. She hated the deceitful wretch. Yet he had taught her to follow her instincts in the wild and this had saved her from disaster on her earlier adventures away from the farm.

'Go away, Sly One! You can't help. It's useless. Myrtle is doomed.'

'Come on, that's not the Mauby I know - the fearless cat whose ancestors stalked the African jungle. This is most unusual. You never give up, Mauby. What's wrong?'

'I tell you, it's hopeless. What can I, a little cat, do against the full might of a Hurricane?'

'Well, I wouldn't call you "little". More like "fat",' chuckled Sly One.

Mauby gave him an angry stare and looked even more miserable.

'Instincts, Mauby, God gave you instincts, not to mention brains. Use them!'

Mauby was about to give a sharp answer when she suddenly realised that the river at this point curved in a long S bend. If she went straight ahead across the field to the next bend she might be able to get ahead of Myrtle.

Sly One was of the same mind. They set off together. Luckily they were going with the wind so they reached the next bend quickly.

Myrtle, clinging to her roof, was still upriver.

A little distance away, Mauby saw that a tree on the bank of the river had fallen and most of its trunk was hanging over the river. If she could climb out on to the trunk she might be able to reach down and pluck Myrtle off the roof as it passed under the tree.

The only problem was that the wind was blowing so hard that Mauby was in danger of being blown off the tree into the river. But she had to risk it.

'I'll help you, Mauby,' Sly One volunteered, 'I'll lead the way.'

So saying, Sly One leaped on to the fallen tree and started making his way among the branches along the trunk. Mauby followed.

The branches and leaves provided some shelter from the wind and rain. But even so, several times Mauby almost lost her grip and fell into the churning water. Once she felt the whole tree shake and groan.

Slowly Mauby crept out along the tree, clinging on with all her strength. The roof, tossing and turning in the current, was now rapidly approaching. Myrtle still lay huddled in the hole between the shingles. Mauby could see that the roof would bump into the tree just where she and Sly One were waiting. That would be her one chance to grab Myrtle and pull her to safety.

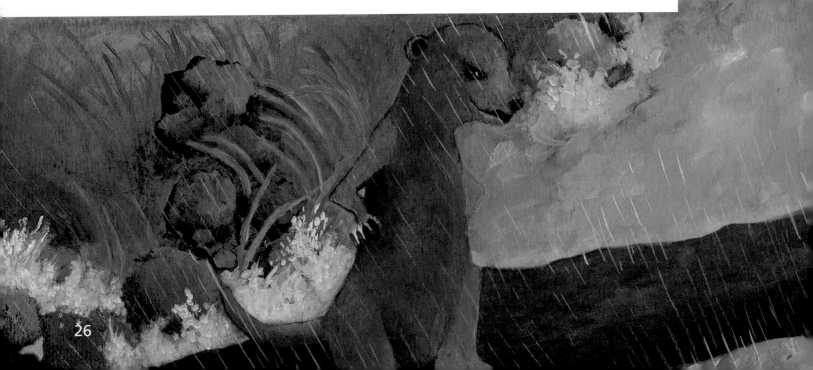

'Mauby', said Sly One, 'I suggest you pass the little hen to me and I'll take her into my den and keep her there safely until the storm is over.'

'Keep her safely?' snorted Mauby. 'The only place you would keep her safely is in your belly. I'm not trusting you with that little hen.'

'Okay, have it your way. I'm off.' Sly One scurried back along the trunk of the tree to the bank of the river.

Suddenly the roof crashed into the tree with a force that almost knocked Mauby into the river.

The fury of the water threatened to smash the roof as it became stuck against the tree. Mauby tried to reach Myrtle, but couldn't.

'Myrtle,' Mauby screamed into the howling wind, 'come here!'

Myrtle didn't budge. She was crouched in her hole, eyes shut tight, head tucked beneath one wing.

Mauby had no choice. She stepped down on to the roof, which was bucking wildly against the current. She dug her claws into the shingles and crept over to the place where Myrtle huddled in fear.

'Myrtle, I've come to rescue you.'

Myrtle opened her eyes. 'M-M-auby!' She flung herself at Mauby, who grabbed her just in time.

Mauby held the little hen in her mouth and tried to jump back onto the tree. But the roof was now swinging wildly about and beginning to break up. Twice Mauby tried and failed. Then the third time she lunged desperately and managed to get her front paws onto the trunk. She pulled herself up.

Lightning flashed, almost blinding her. A clap of thunder followed.

Suddenly the tree began to groan and tremble. The bank on which it lay collapsed and the entire tree fell into the river.

'Instincts, use your instincts!' Mauby heard Sly One's voice above the howling Hurricane, just as the tree was swept out into the river.

Mauby hurriedly shifted her position on the trunk as it spun and turned in the current.

Clutching Myrtle in her mouth, she climbed up to the roots which stuck farthest out of the water. The tree was being taken swiftly down the river to the sea.

Then Mauby remembered that before the river reached the sea it flowed through a gully and fell over the side of a cliff. They would surely be smashed to pieces in the waterfall which they were fast approaching.

In a short while Mauby could hear the roar of the waterfall.

Mauby had almost given up hope when she saw just ahead of her an amazing scene. A troop of monkeys were clinging by their tails from the branch of the baobab tree that grew on the side of the gully just at the top of the waterfall. Mauby's heart filled with joy. It was her good friend Makak and his family who had rescued her from the fierce crocodile, Ligaru, on her last adventure. They were shrieking and clapping their hands as the tree on which Mauby and Myrtle were perched raced towards them.

The roar of the waterfall was now ear-splitting. Mauby could see the white spray that was hurled high into the air as the water crashed over the cliff. Just as they passed under the baobab branch and were about to slide over the fall, Mauby felt Makak's strong hands snatch her and Myrtle to safety.

Makak, holding Mauby and Myrtle, quickly ran along the branch of the baobab tree until he reached the large hollow in the trunk where the sturdy branches met. The other monkeys gathered around.

'You'll be safe here, Mauby,' said Makak, 'until the Hurricane blows over. This baobab tree is the strongest tree in the world. Do you see how thick its trunk is? Also, its roots are stuck firmly in the ground.'

'I can't stay.' said Mauby, 'I must get back to the barn with Myrtle. The other animals will be worried.'

'Mauby,' chided Makak, 'you may be brave, but don't be silly. You're over a mile away from the farm. The Hurricane is now at its peak. You'll never make it back.'

'Hey, maybe I can help.' A small voice came from below the tree. Looking down, they saw Clipper the crab peering out of a hole near to the trunk of the tree. She waved a blue claw at them.

35

'Hi, Clipper, great to see you,' Mauby shouted with delight. Clipper was another good friend who had helped her on her previous adventures. 'How're you doing?'

'Oh, Hurricanes don't bother me. I can lie low in one of my many holes, and the wetter the better. But look, Mauby, if you must get back to the farm, I know a secret way I discovered by chance. There's an old tunnel that runs from the farm right down next to this waterfall. The entrance is blocked up but there is a small hole you can squeeze through. The tunnel is quite big. It was used by smugglers in the old days to bring barrels of wine up to the farm from the beach where they landed their boats at night.'

Mauby did not like the sound of this at all. It was not only that she had a fear of heights, but she also hated being underground in the dark.

'Maybe the tunnel is blocked up,' she suggested.

'No, I have passed through it right up to the farm.' said Clipper.

'Where does the tunnel come out at the farm?' Mauby asked.

'Right in the barn. There's a trap door in the floor.'

'So how do you expect me to open the trap door?'

'Just shout and the other animals in the barn will open it for you.'

'I don't know,' said Mauby, 'What do you think, Makak?'

'I know all about the tunnel, Mauby,' Makak paused and scratched his head. 'But I didn't suggest it. You see, there is one problem. In the middle of the tunnel there is a cave which you have to pass through ...'

'A cave can't be any worse than a tunnel,' said Mauby, recalling her quest for the magic flower in the crocodile's cave.

'Yes,' said Makak, 'but in this cave there is a small colony of vampire bats, led by a mean, vicious old bat called Vlad. He just loves to suck the blood of mammals.'

Mauby shuddered. The only thing she hated more than a dark tunnel was a dark tunnel with a blood-sucking bat in it.

'Perhaps the tunnel's not such a good idea,' said Mauby.

'I want to go home,' wailed Myrtle, ruffling her feathers, 'I want my Mommy.'

'Oh shut up, you stupid little chicken! It's your fault we're here now and not in a nice warm barn with all the other animals.'

'Well,' said Clipper, 'the good thing is that the bats will be asleep now since it's daytime. They hang from the roof of the cave by their feet. If you pass through the cave quietly and don't disturb them they won't even know you're there.'

'Besides,' added Makak, 'I'll give you some special herbs to wear around your neck. They ward off vampires and all kinds of evil spirits. I know they work because we monkeys use them all the time.' He reached into a hole in the tree and took out a string of herbs, which he tied around Mauby's neck.

'Yuck!' exclaimed Mauby, 'I know how they work. They smell so stink that no other creature will come near you.' The monkeys shrieked with laughter.

Makak and Clipper showed Mauby where the entrance to the tunnel was in the hillside next to the waterfall.

Getting from the baobab tree to the tunnel was not easy. The rain had stopped but the wind was still strong. Coconut trees swayed wildly back and forth. They could hear the surf pounding on the beach down below, sending white foam flying into the air.

Mauby, helped by Clipper, Makak and the other monkeys, scratched at the tiny hole until it was large enough for her to enter. Saying goodbye to her friends, Mauby, followed by a squawking Myrtle, squeezed through the hole into the tunnel.

Inside, it was dark except for the little light that came from the hole. Mauby noticed how quiet it was. The storm was now merely a murmur. Mauby felt Myrtle jump onto her back. She shook her off.

'Listen, Myrtle, I'm not carrying you. Stop your cackling and walk right behind me.'

They had taken only a few steps when Mauby tripped over Myrtle.

'I said walk behind me, not in front of me.'

'But I can't see. I'm afraid.' screeched Myrtle.

'Just hold my tail in your beak and follow me. That ought to keep you quiet.'

Like all cats Mauby could see in the dark and she had no difficulty in following the tunnel. She didn't like the musty smell, but at least the tunnel was fairly big.

After a few minutes Mauby smelt something unpleasant. The nasty odour got worse as they went on.

'What's that stinky smell?' Myrtle asked. Her voice broke the silence like a glass shattering.

'Shut up!' hissed Mauby. 'It's bat dung. We must be getting near the cave. So no more talking,' whispered Mauby.

Mauby realised the tunnel was getting higher.
Suddenly they were at the entrance of a large cave.
The stink was unbearable. Mauby stopped. She
peered up but could see nothing. She listened. It was
silent except for a faint rustling and an occasional
squeak.

Slowly, cautiously, Mauby crept across the cave to
the tunnel on the other side. The ground was slimy.
A thick stinky mush was everywhere. Then Mauby
felt something move under her foot. The ground
was alive with squiggly little creatures. Dung beetles.
Thousands of them. They began to swarm all over
her.

Myrtle gave a loud screech. Mauby looked up.
The ceiling of the cave had come alive with tiny little
points of light. Bats' eyes. At the centre of them was
a larger pair of red eyes that glinted evilly.

Mauby checked to see that the string of herbs was
still tied around her neck. It had fallen off.

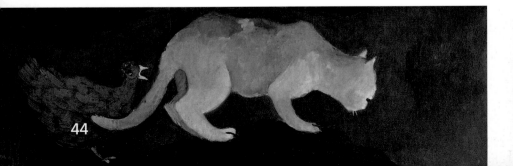

'Come, Myrtle, we're getting out of here!' She grabbed Myrtle in her mouth, none too gently, and took off across the cave and into the tunnel on the other side. She paused to shake off some beetles, and then fled up the tunnel as fast as she could run.

Mauby heard a rushing wind behind her as hundreds of bloodthirsty bats beat their wings in pursuit. She put her head down and ran faster. She felt the fluttering of a thousand wings behind her.

One enormous bat swooped down in front of her. She twisted and darted here and there but the bat continued to swoop and dive in her path, causing her to slow down. The bat suddenly landed ahead of Mauby on a rock that had fallen in the centre of the tunnel, next to a long log.

Mauby screeched to a stop, just feet away from the bat. Vlad's long wings were spread out above his head. Two oversized pointed ears, fierce red eyes and a pair of long sharp teeth were his fearsome features.

'Now, just where do you think you're going?' The high-pitched grating voice made Mauby's hair stand on end. She put Myrtle on the ground so she could catch her breath.

Mauby noticed that drops of water were falling from the roof of the tunnel just above the rock on which Vlad squatted.

'Lost your tongue, cat? Or just scared out of your wits? I'm glad you ran so fast. It makes your blood grow thin and easier to suck.' Vlad made a horrible chuckling, slurping sound. He was joined by the other bats that now surrounded Mauby. The tunnel was filled with their high-pitched squeaks.

Mauby shivered. Myrtle squawked.

The drops of water had become a trickle.

'My followers can have that scrawny chicken, but I think I'll feast on you, you nice fat cat: I'm v-e-r-y, v-e-r-y thirsty.' Vlad bared his teeth and flew at Mauby.

Mauby swiftly sidestepped and backed up against one side of the tunnel. Myrtle ran under Mauby's tummy and hid her head beneath her wing. Instinctively, Mauby stood as tall as she could on her legs, arched her back, bared her own teeth and claws and hissed as loudly as she could.

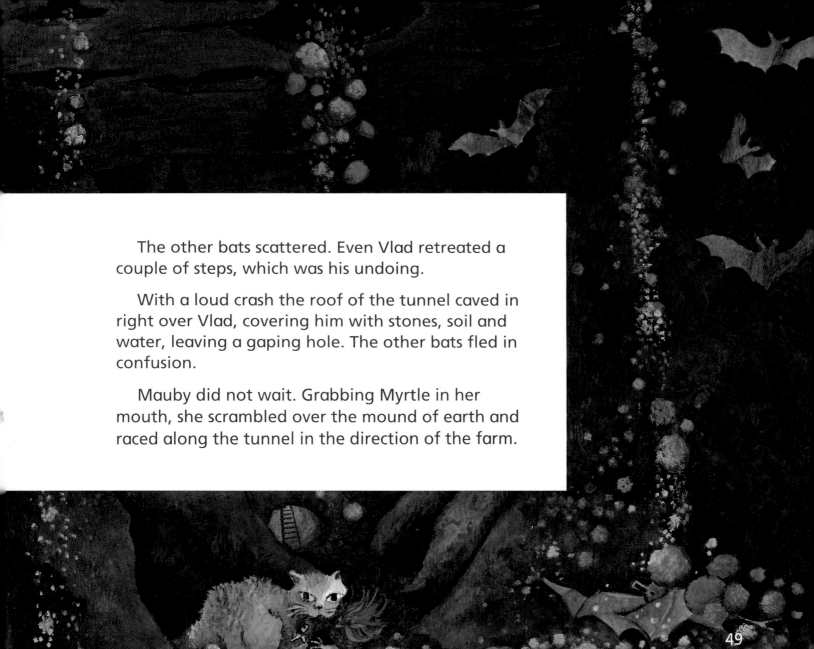

The other bats scattered. Even Vlad retreated a couple of steps, which was his undoing.

With a loud crash the roof of the tunnel caved in right over Vlad, covering him with stones, soil and water, leaving a gaping hole. The other bats fled in confusion.

Mauby did not wait. Grabbing Myrtle in her mouth, she scrambled over the mound of earth and raced along the tunnel in the direction of the farm.

She ran so fast that she bumped into the wall where the tunnel abruptly came to an end. There was a ladder whose iron rungs were embedded in the wall. 'This must lead up to the barn,' thought Mauby.

She climbed up the ladder, still holding Myrtle in her mouth.

There was a wide ledge. Mauby scrambled onto it. She put Myrtle down and looked around her. A set of wooden steps led from the ledge to a trap door above. Mauby climbed up the steps and put her ear to the trap door. She could hear animals talking.

Mauby gave a loud cry, but the noises above did not stop. She shouted even louder. But no one could hear her. What was she to do? The trap door was too heavy for her to push open.

Just then Mauby heard a loud hoot. Looking around, she saw Boo land on the ledge.

'Boo! Thank God you're here! I can't get the trap door open, and the animals in the barn can't hear me … by the way, how did you get here? How did you know we were here? Is there another way out of the tunnel?'

'One question at a time, Mauby,' said Boo. 'I saw you get carried off by the river to the falls. We owls have known about the tunnel for a long time, and I had a hunch you might use it to get back. As luck would have it, the tunnel caved in not far from here, so I flew into to it and made my way here.'

'But weren't you afraid of Vlad and the bats?'

'Bats are just smelly rats with wings, Mauby. Don't forget that I eat rats and mice. I admit that Vlad is a fairly big rat, but he's still no match for me. Haven't you noticed that the vampire bats don't come near this farm? That's because I keep an eye out for them. By the way, what happened to Vlad?'

'The sky fell on him,' said Mauby.

'You can tell me about it later,' said Boo. 'The Hurricane is almost over. I'll fly back to the barn and tell the other animals to let you in.'

Boo flew off down the tunnel.

52

In a few minutes' time the trap door flew open and there were Bongo, Gamps, Shakes, Tiki-Tak and Myra peering down at Mauby and Myrtle. Mauby gathered up Myrtle and quickly climbed through the trap door into the barn.

All the animals gave shouts of joy when they saw Mauby and Myrtle.

Soon the barn was filled with noise as all the animals talked at the top of their voices at the same time.

'Shut up!' screamed Mauby. When the noise stopped, Mauby told them what had happened to her and Myrtle. 'And I want you all to know,' she said, 'that this is absolutely the last time I am ever setting foot outside of this farm. In fact I shall ask farmer Hunte if I can become a house cat.'

'Oh, no, Mauby,' shouted Bongo and Tiki-Tak together, 'we would miss you too much. Besides, you are quite a famous adventurer now.' Tiki-Tak and Bongo exchanged sly glances and smiled. But before Mauby could get out her angry reply, there was a loud hoot from the rafters of the barn.

'The Hurricane has blown over,' said Boo. 'I think I hear Farmer Hunte's truck. It's safe to go outside now.'

The animals rushed out of the barn just as Farmer Hunte and his wife drove into the yard. They got out and looked in amazement at all the animals gathered outside the barn door.

He shook his head, smiled and said to his wife, 'Somehow, I think Mauby had something to do with this, but I guess we'll never know.' They walked around the farm seeing what damage had been done. They were followed by all the animals except Mauby.

Mauby had curled herself up in her favourite spot by the water trough and gone fast asleep.

Macmillan Education
Between Towns Road, Oxford OX4 3PP
A division of Macmillan Publishers Limited
Companies and representatives throughout the world

www.macmillan-caribbean.com

ISBN-13: 978-1-4050-7718-7

Designed by Carol Hulme
Illustrated by H. Ann Dodson
Cover design by Bob Swan

Printed in Thailand

2011 2010 2009 2008 2007
10 9 8 7 6 5 4 3 2 1

To teacher Kerry Howard and the children of
the 2004 Class 1 at Vauxhall Primary School for
inspiring this third Mauby story.